Johnny Appleseed and the BEARS

written by
David Novak

illustrated by
David Wenzel

What is the house that is round and red,
without window or door, table or bed?
What house has a chimney on the top,
when the chimney breaks, the house will drop?
What house is it, when opened wide,
shows a star or two inside?
That house is an apple.

I dedicate this book to the new age of storytelling and to the old storytelling traditions that are still with us. I also dedicate this book to the many storytelling festivals across the United States that have helped further my work—in particular, the Northern Appalachian Storytelling Festival in Mansfield, Pennsylvania, and the Allen County Storytelling Festival in Fort Wayne, Indiana, where I first thought of this story.

Published by Riverbank Press
801 94th Avenue North, St. Petersburg, Florida 33702

Copyright © 1995 by Riverbank Press, a division of PAGES, Inc.

Printed in the United States of America

2 4 6 8 10 9 7 5 3

ISBN 0-87406-782-0

How *Johnny Appleseed and the Bears* Came to Be

There are many stories of the adventurous fellow John Chapman, better known as Johnny Appleseed. He traveled from Pennsylvania through Ohio, Indiana, and Illinois during the early 1800s, planting apple seeds for the pioneers. He died in Fort Wayne, Indiana, and his grave can be found there at Johnny Appleseed Park.

Johnny was said to be quite a storyteller, and he made a practice of planting stories as well as seeds. His two favorite books were the Bible and *Aesop's Fables*.

Characters like Johnny Appleseed have long been an inspiration to storytellers like me. *Johnny Appleseed and the Bears* is my original contribution to a long and lively tradition of tales about American folk heroes.

— *David Novak*

One sunny day in early October, Johnny Appleseed hiked up to a wide mountain meadow. He carried a sack full of bright red apples, fresh-picked from one of his apple orchards. Today was his day for cutting out seeds. Later he would plant the seeds for the people he visited. When the seeds grew into trees, the people would have fresh apples to eat.

Johnny leaned against a sun-warmed rock in the middle of that bright meadow. He took out his paring knife and began slicing open apples. Then he took out the seeds.

The trees were ablaze with autumn colors. The air was fresh and cool. This was just the sort of place Johnny considered to be heaven on earth. So as he worked, he made up a song:

How happy I am to sit in the sun
With bright autumn colors and a cool autumn breeze.
I'm doing the work that needs to be done
With apples I've grown from my own apple trees!

Johnny thought he heard something growl.
He listened.

Everything was quiet. So Johnny went back to work.

GRRRRRR!!

There it was again! A growling GRRRRR!! Johnny looked up.

At the edge of the woods he could see a dark shadow. Out of that shadow stuck a black, shiny nose. Attached to that nose was a big black bear!

Johnny knew a thing or two about bears. Johnny knew that bears sleep in the winter and don't wake up until spring. Johnny knew that autumn is the time when bears are always eating, to get ready for their long winter sleep. Johnny also knew that bears will eat anything. They might even eat Johnny Appleseed!

Papa Bear started coming toward him! But Johnny didn't panic. He said, "Papa Bear, how would you like an apple? Apples are sweet and sugary. They taste better than any scrawny old Johnny Appleseed."

Johnny reached into his sack, sliced open an apple, and took out the seeds. Then he tossed the rest of the apple to Papa Bear.

Papa Bear picked up that apple and munched on it. Then he nodded, as if to say, "Thank you kindly!"

Johnny said, "Don't mention it, friend. I'm glad to be of service!"

Papa Bear turned around and walked off into the woods.

Everything was quiet. So Johnny went back to work.
Suddenly he heard *two* growls!

There were *two* black bears: Papa Bear and Mama Bear.
Well, Johnny had plenty of apples. He reached into his sack, sliced some open, and took out the seeds. Then he tossed the apples to the bears.

Papa Bear and Mama Bear ate the apples, nodded to Johnny, and walked away. Everything was quiet. So Johnny went back to work.

Three growls!

There was Papa Bear, Mama Bear, and Baby Bear! Once again, Johnny reached into his sack, sliced open some apples, and took out the seeds. Then he tossed the apples to the bears. Once again, the bears ate the apples, nodded to Johnny, and walked away.

Things weren't very quiet after that. Along came Papa Bear, Mama Bear, Baby Bear, Grandpa Bear, Grandma Bear, Aunt Bear, Uncle Bear, and Cousin Bear!
And more bears were still coming!

Soon all of the bears on that mountain came into the meadow for a big bear picnic.

Over and over again, Johnny reached into his sack, sliced open some apples, and took out the seeds. Then he tossed the apples to the bears. He was afraid he might run out of apples. But he kept finding more and more apples in his sack.

Finally all of the bears were full. They stretched out in that meadow and looked at Johnny with big, shining black eyes.
"I wonder what they want now?" thought Johnny.

Then he understood. Those bears had to wear the same furry suit of clothes all the time. They were bound to itch!

So Johnny stepped among the bears, giving them scratches. The bears stretched and yawned. One by one, they fell asleep.

Everything was quiet.

Johnny Appleseed stood in the middle of that meadow, watching those dozing bears. He watched for a long time.

Then he thought, "I have to travel on, and I'm not likely to be back this way again. I wonder who will be here next year to feed the bears and scratch their backs? I plant my apple seeds for the people to eat, but I suppose I can spare a few for the bears."

So Johnny stepped among the bears once more. This time he planted seeds—one for each bear. Finally he picked up his sack and tiptoed away.

That was a long time ago, and Johnny Appleseed has long since left this world. But his apple trees are still here.

There is a mountain meadow in the northern Appalachian range with a wild apple orchard growing in it. If you go there in the autumn, you're likely to find a black bear or two munching on apples and rubbing up against those trees. For after all these years, Johnny Appleseed still feeds the bears, and scratches their backs!

About the Author

David Novak

David Novak has been a professional storyteller since 1978. He has told stories to audiences all over the country, and has appeared at the International Reading Association conference in Toronto, the Shorebird Festival in Alaska, Los Marineros Marine Educators conference in California, Stories Alive! in Iowa, and the Stone Soup Festival in South Carolina. He has also been a featured teller at the National Storytelling Festival in Jonesborough, Tennessee.

Telling stories in front of audiences is only part of what David does, however. In addition to producing two cassettes of stories, he has produced several programs for the Lincoln Center Institute in New York and the Los Angeles Music Center on Tour. He has also taught at the International Storytelling Institute at Eastern Tennessee State University and at numerous state library conferences.

David's background includes many years of fine arts education and professional experience in the theater. He lives in San Diego, California, with his wife, Courtney, his son, Jack, one dog, one cat, and lots of stories.

Johnny Appleseed and the Bears is his second book for Riverbank Press.

About the Illustrator

David Wenzel

David Wenzel is known for the folk and fairy tale worlds he creates with pen, pencil, and watercolor. His illustrations have appeared in numerous children's books including *Kingdom of the Dwarfs, Hauntings,* and *Backyard Dragon.* He has been recognized worldwide for his graphic novel adaptation of J.R.R. Tolkien's *The Hobbit.*

David lives in the Connecticut countryside with his wife, Janice, two sons, and their pet pig, Gus. From his hilltop studio he works on his illustrations and collaborates on projects based on his concept of The Hidden Kingdom, a fantasy world of fairy folk who work at playing by celebrating a holiday three hundred and sixty-five days a year.